Meet Bob Wakefield!

"You want to interview us about being twins?" Jessica asked eagerly.

Ms. Loomis nodded. "That's right. When I heard that your family has *two* sets of identical twins, I just couldn't resist finding out more."

Elizabeth's nervous, floating feeling began to feel like a bagful of butterflies banging around in her stomach. But maybe Ms. Loomis wouldn't ask too many questions.

"Now, you're Bob, right?" Ms. Loomis asked Steven.

Steven nodded. "Umm, yes, I'm Bob, and Steven is—um . . ." His voice trailed off.

"In the bathroom," Elizabeth blurted out.

"Well, when he joins us, I'll feel like I'm just seeing double everywhere I look," Ms. Loomis said with a laugh.

Bantam Books in the SWEET VALLEY KIDS series

SWEET VALLEY KIDS

STEVEN'S TWIN

Written by
Molly Mia Stewart

Created by
FRANCINE PASCAL

Illustrated by
Ying-Hwa Hu

BANTAM BOOKS
NEW YORK·TORONTO·LONDON·SYDNEY·AUCKLAND

RL 2, 005-008

STEVEN'S TWIN
A Bantam Book / July 1994

*Sweet Valley High® and Sweet Valley Kids are
trademarks of Francine Pascal*

Conceived by Francine Pascal

*Produced by Daniel Weiss Associates, Inc.
33 West 17th Street
New York, NY 10011*

Cover art by Susan Tang

ISBN: 0-553-48095-2

Published simultaneously in the United States and Canada

*Bantam Books are published by Bantam Books, a division of Bantam
Doubleday Dell Publishing Group, Inc. Its trademark, consisting of the
words "Bantam Books" and the portrayal of a rooster, is Registered in
U.S. Patent and Trademark Office and in other countries. Marca
Registrada. Bantam Books, 1540 Broadway, New York, New York 10036.*

PRINTED IN THE UNITED STATES OF AMERICA

CWO   0 9 8 7 6 5 4 3 2 1

To Ethan Arlook

CHAPTER 1

Twin Delight

"Can't we just skip lunch and go straight to Casey's for dessert?" Elizabeth Wakefield asked with a hopeful smile. Casey's was an ice-cream parlor in Sweet Valley.

Her twin sister, Jessica, gave their mother an identical smile. "I second that suggestion."

"Fat chance," Mrs. Wakefield said, placing a plate full of tuna sandwiches on the table.

Elizabeth and Jessica each picked up a sandwich at the same time and took a bite in the same way. They did many things exactly alike, because they weren't just twins, they were *identical* twins. Both girls had long blond hair with bangs and bluish-green eyes. When they wore matching clothes, it was extra difficult to tell them apart. Even their best friends in second grade had to look at the pretty name bracelets each twin wore to be sure who was who.

But Elizabeth and Jessica were identical only on the outside. Inside, each girl had her own special personality. Elizabeth loved reading and playing all kinds of sports. She was particularly proud to be on the Sweet Valley Soccer League. She paid attention in school and dreamed of being a writer.

Jessica was just the opposite. She liked playing with her dollhouse and watching television. Her favorite part of the school day was recess, and she passed a lot of notes to her friends in class. Jessica loved being the center of attention. So no one was surprised that she dreamed of being a movie star.

But even though they were different on the inside, Elizabeth and Jessica were still best friends. They shared a bedroom, clothes, and toys. Sometimes they could even complete each other's sentences. That was because identical twins shared a special kind of understanding. Their older brother, Steven, often teased them about being two of a kind, but Elizabeth and Jessica thought being twins was the greatest thing in the world.

Elizabeth took another bite from her sandwich and put it down on the plate at the exact moment that Jessica did. Both girls grinned.

"I bet you're sorry you aren't a twin today," Jessica said to Steven.

Steven shrugged and picked out a carrot stick from a dish full of raw vegetables. "So you get a free ice-cream sundae, big deal."

"You're just jealous," Elizabeth said with a laugh. "Today is Twin Delight day and you're left out."

Casey's Ice Cream Parlor was introducing a new ice-cream sundae, Twin Sundae Delight. To get people to come, the manager had handed out flyers all over Sweet Valley and nearby towns. The flyers invited all identical twins to come that afternoon for a free sundae. Newspaper reporters, photographers, and most of all, lots and lots of identical twins were coming.

"I bet it isn't even a good sundae," Steven decided.

Jessica shook her head so hard her ponytail swung back and forth under her bright-orange baseball cap. "No way. You get four scoops of two different kinds of

ice cream, chocolate syrup with peanut-butter swirl, some pineapple sauce, colored sprinkles, mounds of whipped cream, chocolate shavings, and a maraschino cherry smack on top."

"Stop!" Steven put his hands over his ears. "It sounds awful."

"Oh, really? It sounds pretty good to me," Mr. Wakefield said.

"Me, too," Elizabeth agreed. "But Steven doesn't get one. He's just a single-scoop-on-a-cone person."

Everyone at the table laughed, but Steven waved his carrot stick at Elizabeth. "Just you wait. I'll get a free ice-cream sundae somehow."

"You'd have to go through a science-fiction twin-making machine for that to happen," Jessica told him. She made a face. "And then we'll have two Stevens. Yuck!"

Everyone laughed again except for

6

Steven. He just smiled a mysterious smile and finished his lunch.

"Now, who's ready for a free Twin Sundae Delight?" Mrs. Wakefield asked.

Elizabeth and Jessica jumped up at the same time. *"Me!"* they shouted.

"Race you to the car," Elizabeth told Jessica.

In a few moments, the whole family was in the Wakefield station wagon. Elizabeth began listing her favorite ice-cream flavors.

"Chocolate marshmallow, vanilla Swiss almond—" she began.

"Oreo mint vanilla, mocha chocolate chip," Jessica finished. She and Elizabeth always chose between those four flavors.

Steven folded his arms across his chest and frowned as he looked out the window.

"Steven, I'll give you some money for ice cream," Mr. Wakefield promised as they pulled up in front of Casey's. "Mom and I will drop you kids off so we can do some errands, but we'll pick you up in about half an hour. OK?"

Elizabeth and Jessica bounced on their seats. "OK!"

Steven took two dollars from Mr. Wakefield and put it in his pocket.

"Too bad you have to pay for yours," Jessica teased.

Steven climbed out of the car. "I'm going to have ice cream," he said confidently. "And it's going to be free."

Elizabeth laughed. "How are you going to do that?"

"Just watch," Steven said. "Prepare to be amazed."

CHAPTER 2

Steven's Plan

Jessica grabbed Elizabeth's hand. "Ignore him," she said, running to the door of the ice-cream parlor. "Let's get our sundaes."

The moment they entered Casey's, Jessica and Elizabeth stopped in astonishment. The place was filled with twins of all ages, from babies in double strollers to gray-haired men and women. There were several photographers, as well as plenty of extra family members enjoying the spectacle.

"Look at all the identical twins!" Jessica

gasped as they stood in line behind two redheaded boys with freckles and identical kung-fu T-shirts. "I've never seen so many."

"Hello," said a man behind the counter. "Welcome to Casey's Twin Sundae Delight. I'm the new manager, Mr. Bixby."

"Are you an identical twin, too?" Elizabeth asked him.

Mr. Bixby chuckled. "I sure am, but my twin lives in Ohio. I should have asked him to come visit. Looks like twins from far away showed up. What two flavors of ice cream would you like for your Twin Delight sundaes?"

At the same instant both girls replied, "Chocolate marshmallow, Oreo mint vanilla."

"Identical twins, no doubt about it," Mr. Bixby said with a laugh. "My brother and I used to yell 'jinx' anytime we said the same word at the same time."

"I guess we'd have to say jinx all the time, then," Elizabeth decided.

While Mr. Bixby was busy preparing their sundaes, Jessica looked for Steven. She spotted him eyeing all the ice-cream flavors behind the glass case. "What flavor ice-cream cone are you getting?" Jessica asked when he came over.

"I'm not getting anything—yet," Steven said. "But I'll find us a table before they're all filled." He smiled another mysterious smile and walked off.

"Don't pay any attention to him," Elizabeth whispered to Jessica. "He just wants us to ask what his plan is." She shook her head. "As if he has one."

Grinning, Jessica nodded in agreement. She watched eagerly as Mr. Bixby sprayed mounds of whipped cream on their sundaes and then topped each one off with a cherry.

"Here you go," the manager said. "Enjoy!"

11

"Thank you," Jessica said. She carried them carefully to the table where Steven was sitting. Elizabeth brought two cups of water, two spoons, and two napkins, and sat beside her.

"They look super delicious," Jessica said. She scooped some whipped cream with one finger and licked it off. "Umm, umm, good! Don't you wish you had a twin now, Steven?"

Suddenly a wide, triumphant smile spread across Steven's face. "I do."

"That's news to me," Elizabeth said, digging her spoon into her ice-cream sundae.

"No, seriously," Steven said. "Let's pretend I'm an identical twin so I can get a Twin Sundae Delight, too."

"But there's only one of you," Elizabeth pointed out. "In case you hadn't noticed."

Jessica giggled. She held the cherry above her mouth and plucked it off its

12

stem with her teeth. "You couldn't get away with it in a million years," she said as she chewed.

"I bet I could," Steven insisted. His eyes were sparkling with excitement. He leaned across the table and lowered his voice. "But you two have to help me. Will you do it?"

Jessica smiled. She loved practical jokes, and she was curious to see if Steven could pull off being a twin. "It would be an excellent trick if we could do it," she said slowly.

"I don't know," Elizabeth said, shaking her head. "And besides, it's like stealing from Mr. Bixby. He was nice to us."

"Come on, Elizabeth," Steven begged. "It'll be fun. And I'll come back later and give Mr. Bixby the money. Honest."

"We won't hurt anyone," Jessica told Elizabeth. "Say you'll help, Liz."

Elizabeth licked hot fudge off her spoon

and shrugged. "I'll help, but I have a feeling something will go wrong. It always does. Anytime you and I switch places, Jessica, we end up getting in some kind of trouble."

"Don't be a spoilsport," Steven said.

"Yeah, either people will believe Steven or they won't. Forget about trouble schrouble," Jessica said.

Steven nodded, but Elizabeth shook her head again. "I am completely, positively sure something will go wrong," she said. "But I'll help."

"Well, if something does go wrong, then Steven has to do our chores for a week," Jessica announced. She looked right at Steven. "And if nothing goes wrong and you get free sundaes, you have to share one of them with us."

"It's a deal," Steven said, smiling from ear to ear. He leaned across the table. "Now, here's what we do. . . ."

CHAPTER 3

Twice the Trouble

"I don't know about this," Elizabeth muttered, following Steven to the counter.

"How's the sundae?" asked the manager when he saw Elizabeth return.

"It was delicious," Elizabeth said. "I finished the whole thing." She crossed her fingers behind her back. "But my brother didn't get his Twin Sundae Delight yet."

Mr. Bixby raised his eyebrows in surprise. "You're a twin, too?" he asked Steven.

"Yes," Steven answered.

Elizabeth crossed her toes inside her sneakers. She hated lying. And she was sure Mr. Bixby was going to know they weren't telling the truth.

"So where's your brother?" the manager continued.

Steven waved one hand toward the door. "Bob's outside. He'll be in in a second."

Elizabeth looked at Steven. She thought she would burst out laughing. Bob was Steven's best friend, and the real Bob looked totally different from Steven. She covered her mouth with one hand and pretended to cough to hide her smile.

"Well, this is just amazing." The manager was shaking his head from side to side. "Two pairs of twins in one family."

"It is hard to believe, isn't it?" Elizabeth said with a grin.

Steven nudged her with his foot, but Elizabeth was afraid to look at him a second time. She couldn't stop thinking about the real Bob, and how different he looked from Steven. No one would ever mistake them for identical twins!

But since the real Bob wasn't there, nobody knew he wasn't Steven's twin. Elizabeth could hardly believe the joke was actually working.

"Well, so what flavors would you like on your Twin Delight sundae?" Mr. Bixby asked Steven.

While Steven told the manager what flavors he wanted, Elizabeth glanced over her shoulder. She saw Jessica watching them, and Elizabeth cautiously gave her a thumbs-up sign.

"Thanks a lot," Steven said as he reached for the towering sundae. "Bob will be right up to get his. He's going to love it."

He turned and walked away from the counter, and Elizabeth followed him. She

18

still couldn't believe everything had gone so smoothly.

"It worked?" Jessica asked, her eyes wide with excitement.

Steven pulled out his chair and sat down. He had a satisfied grin on his face. "Piece of cake," he boasted.

"But now he's expecting to meet your twin brother Bob," Elizabeth said. "How are you going to pull that off?"

"No sweat. We just have to wait for the right moment," Steven said. "Round one was a piece of cake. Round two will be a piece of cake, too."

He watched over his shoulder until the manager was busy with a crowd of people at the counter. Then he stretched one arm across the table and took Jessica's baseball cap off her head. He pulled it down over his forehead and then took off his plaid shirt so that he was wearing only a T-shirt.

"OK, let's go," he told Jessica.

Elizabeth watched as Steven and Jessica slipped out of the ice-cream parlor.

"I have a funny feeling about this," Elizabeth said under her breath.

She knew perfectly well that when there were twins, there was *twice* as much chance for trouble.

CHAPTER 4

Call Me Bob

Jessica and Steven stood outside the ice-cream shop for a moment to go over the plan one more time.

"I'll go in and ask for my Twin Sundae Delight," Steven said, adjusting the cap on his head. "And we'll see if Mr. Bixby gives me another one."

Jessica smiled, but she knew she had to keep a perfectly straight face. "This is the funniest trick," she whispered. "I feel like a spy."

"Come on," Steven said, nodding toward the door. "And no matter what happens, don't forget to call me Bob."

Jessica giggled. "OK, Bob."

She followed Steven as he walked back into Casey's and went right up to the counter. Steven was very confident. He smiled at Mr. Bixby. "Hi, I'm here for a Twin Sundae Delight. My sister told me my twin brother already got his."

"That's right," the manager said. He looked at Steven closely and scratched his head. "Being a twin, I know how hard it can be to tell twins apart. But you two boys—if I didn't know better, I'd say there's just one of you."

Steven laughed. "I do look *a lot* like Steven," he said truthfully. "Everybody says so."

Jessica swallowed as Mr. Bixby looked out into the ice-cream parlor. She was glad the place was still crowded and that people were gathering right in back of them. If they were lucky, it would be im-

possible for Mr. Bixby to see that Elizabeth was alone at their table.

She glanced at Steven and could tell that he was nervous, too. But then Mr. Bixby shrugged.

"Guess I'm being foolish," he said. "Twins are supposed to look alike, right? So what Sundae Delight flavors would you like?"

"Chocolate fudge chip and maple walnut," Steven said, trying to smile. "Just like my twin."

Jessica was really glad Steven's joke was working so well. She didn't want to get into trouble—not now when they were about to get *another* sundae.

"Almost nobody can tell them apart," Jessica agreed, trying hard not to giggle. "Liz and I are a teeny, tiny bit different if you know what to look for. But Steven and Bob, they're just exactly one hundred percent completely identical."

24

"That's right," Steven said with a nod. "Most people who don't know about Bob think I *am* Steven."

"And you should see them when they play tricks on people," Jessica continued, getting into the spirit of the joke. "Nobody can tell them apart."

Everyone lined up behind them was listening and smiling. Jessica loved being the center of attention, so she decided to add more details to the story.

"Since we have two sets of twins in our family, things get pretty confusing at home, too," she went on cheerfully.

Steven took the sundae from Mr. Bixby. "Thanks," he said. He turned to Jessica. "Let's go eat," he said, trying to get Jessica to move.

But Jessica didn't want to go, because even more people were gathering around. She felt just like an actress onstage.

"You have two pairs of identical twins

25

in one family?" a young woman with chin-length brown hair asked.

"That's right," Jessica said. She sighed dramatically. "And let me tell you. It can get pretty crazy. Bob, remember when you and Steven told the student teacher that you were Steven and he was you?" She and Elizabeth had played that joke themselves.

"That was a long time ago," Steven said. He nudged Jessica forward. But she still didn't move.

"Bob and Steven kept switching places all day long," Jessica explained, smiling up at one face after another. "And Steven, remember how you—"

"I thought he was Bob," the brown-haired woman said.

"Oh, I mean . . ." Jessica laughed breathlessly and slapped her forehead with her hand. "See? Even I get them mixed up."

"Come on, Jessica," Steven said, pulling

26

on her arm. "I want to eat my ice cream before it melts—now."

"OK, *Bob*," Jessica said. "But don't be surprised if Steven already ate his and attacks yours." She smiled at the group around them. "My brothers eat like monsters."

"Very funny," Steven said as he laughed with everyone. Then under his breath he whispered to Jessica, "Quit it now." Steven gave the group around them a friendly smile and then hustled Jessica away.

CHAPTER 5

Celebrity Twins

Elizabeth watched Jessica and Steven walk toward her through the crowded ice-cream parlor. She could see that they both had wide grins on their faces. They both sat down and then burst into laughter behind their hands.

"What took you so long?" Elizabeth asked, looking from Steven to Jessica and back again. "I was sure Mr. Bixby was onto your joke."

"So did I, but we sure fooled him," Jessica said. "It was so much fun."

"Except Jessica nearly blew the whole

thing," Steven said. He dug into his ice-cream sundae. With his mouth full of whipped cream he added, "She called me Steven."

"I told you something would go wrong," Elizabeth said.

Jessica shook her head. "But everyone makes that kind of mistake, so it doesn't matter. They still think he's Steven's twin brother, Bob."

With a satisfied smile Jessica reached across the table and pulled Steven's first sundae toward her and Elizabeth.

"Hey, what are you doing?" Steven said. "Hands off."

"You've got to share," Jessica said, digging in with her spoon. "That's our reward. You promised. Come on, Liz."

Elizabeth started to help devour the sundae when she saw a young brown-haired woman headed their way. The woman was carrying a notebook and a pencil.

"Excuse me," the woman said. "I was talking to you kids up at the front, remember?"

"Sure," Jessica said with a smile. "I remember."

"I hope you don't mind my barging in, but I'm a reporter for the *Sweet Valley News*. My name is Andrea Loomis. I'm covering Casey's Twin Delight day for the paper. I was hoping I could talk to you kids for a couple of minutes."

Elizabeth began to get a nervous, floating feeling in her stomach. She glanced at Steven and tried to shake her head a tiny bit.

But Elizabeth was too late.

"Sure," Jessica said eagerly. "You want to interview us about being twins?"

Ms. Loomis nodded. "That's right. When I heard that your family has *two* sets of identical twins, I just couldn't resist finding out more."

Elizabeth's nervous, floating feeling began to feel like a bagful of butterflies banging around in her stomach. But maybe Ms. Loomis wouldn't ask too many questions.

"Now, you're Bob, right?" Ms. Loomis asked Steven. She was writing very fast in her notebook, faster than Elizabeth had ever seen anyone write.

Steven nodded, and his eyes darted to Elizabeth. "Umm, yes, I'm Bob, and Steven is—um . . ." His voice trailed off.

"In the bathroom," Elizabeth blurted out.

"Well, when he joins us, I'll feel like I'm just seeing double everywhere I look," Ms. Loomis said with a laugh.

"He might be a long time," Steven said uncomfortably. "He's not feeling well." Steven began eating his ice cream as fast as he could, shoveling it into his mouth.

Elizabeth took a sip of water and stared

at her empty dish. She was very embarrassed.

"Are you a television reporter?" Jessica asked Ms. Loomis.

"No, just for the newspaper," Ms. Loomis said. "Tell me, how do your parents feel about having two sets of identical twins?"

"They don't mind," Elizabeth mumbled.

"Oh, come on, Liz. They love it!" Jessica gushed. She watched Ms. Loomis write down exactly what she had said.

Elizabeth wished Jessica didn't love attention so much. She was sure Jessica was going to make things even worse.

"I'll tell you what," Ms. Loomis went on. She tapped her chin with her pencil. "I would love to interview your whole family together for a human-interest story. You four twins and your parents. And set up a photographer, too."

"You mean we'd get our pictures in the paper?" Jessica asked in a thrilled voice. "Sure!"

"No!" Elizabeth and Steven shouted.

Ms. Loomis looked surprised. "Why not?"

"They're just shy," Jessica said.

"Jessica!" Elizabeth growled.

But Jessica didn't seem to realize what a huge mistake she had made. When Ms. Loomis asked for their last name and address, Jessica told her instantly.

"I'll come by tomorrow afternoon after lunch," Ms. Loomis said as she stood up to leave. "I hope Steven feels better then. Bye-bye."

" 'Bye," Jessica said cheerfully.

Elizabeth slumped down in her chair. "Thanks a lot, Jessica. Thanks for getting us into a big mess."

CHAPTER 6

Too Late to Back Out

As soon as Ms. Loomis was out of earshot, Steven and Elizabeth turned to Jessica.

"Are you out of your mind?" Steven asked in a high, squeaking voice. "Have you totally and completely lost all of your marbles?"

"Why? What's wrong?" Jessica said, feeling hurt. She looked from Steven to Elizabeth. "Don't you want to get our pictures in the newspaper?"

"Pictures of who?" Elizabeth asked.

"You, me, Steven . . ." Jessica's cheeks

suddenly turned pink from embarrassment.

"And Bob?" Steven demanded. "My identical twin brother Bob?" He yanked the orange baseball cap from his head and slapped it on the table.

Elizabeth began to giggle. Jessica glared at her as she folded her arms and pouted. She felt very foolish, and she hated that feeling more than anything else in the world. Elizabeth certainly wasn't making her feel any better.

"This is the stupidest thing we ever did," Elizabeth finally said. She took a sip of water and then giggled again.

Jessica frowned in concentration; then she licked the last traces of ice cream from her spoon. She was trying to think of a solution. She was determined to get her picture into the paper. There was only one obstacle: Steven did not have a twin brother.

"We'll have to call the newspaper and tell Ms. Loomis it was just a joke," Elizabeth said.

"No way," Steven said instantly.

"No way," Jessica chimed in.

Elizabeth looked startled. "Now you're both crazy," she said, staring at Steven.

"We're not calling it off," Steven insisted stubbornly. "I know exactly what will happen. Mom and Dad will give me a big lecture, and they'll make me apologize in front of a whole bunch of people."

"So?" Elizabeth asked.

"So that would be really embarrassing," Steven growled.

"And besides," Jessica said, "if we call it off, we don't get our picture in the paper."

"But we don't have a brother named Bob!" Elizabeth said. "How can we go through with it and not have anyone finding out the truth?"

Jessica drummed her fingers on the

table. "We'll think of something," she muttered.

"Mom and Dad will never go along with it," Elizabeth pointed out.

"They're not supposed to know about it, anyway," Steven reminded Elizabeth.

"Can't we just tell Ms. Loomis that Steven is still sick?" Jessica said with a hopeful expression. "Or staying over at a friend's house?"

Elizabeth shook her head. "The excuse worked today. But what happens when Ms. Loomis asks Mom and Dad about having *two* sets of twins in the family? That's why she's coming over, remember? Mom and Dad know Steven doesn't have a twin brother."

"I know, I know," Jessica said. "But there's got to be a way."

"I agree," Steven said. "There's got to be a way."

Elizabeth shook her head. "You've both

gone bonkers," she said. "This can't work."

"It can. Trust us. Besides, it's too late to back out now. Promise you'll go along with it, Liz," Jessica begged. "Please please please?"

"Oh, all right," Elizabeth said. "I know I shouldn't, but I will."

"Make the promise sign," Jessica said.

Elizabeth crossed her heart and snapped her fingers three times. That was a special signal between them, and Jessica knew her sister would keep her promise.

"And don't worry," Jessica said. "I'll think of something." She just wasn't sure what.

CHAPTER 7

Mind-boggling

Mr. and Mrs. Wakefield picked up Steven and the twins a few minutes later. Elizabeth was quiet as she climbed into the car behind her sister.

"How was the sundae?" Mrs. Wakefield asked.

"Delicious," Jessica replied. "And guess what."

"What?" their father asked.

"A reporter is coming over tomorrow to interview us," Jessica said happily. "She wants to meet our whole family."

Elizabeth didn't know whether she

wanted to laugh or scream. She just shook her head and looked out the car window.

"Why would a reporter want to interview us?" Mrs. Wakefield asked. "We're pretty run-of-the-mill."

The kids exchanged uncertain looks in the backseat. Steven cleared his throat.

"Umm, it's about—about families with twins," he said. "There was a reporter interviewing twins for the paper. She chose us for a big blurb."

Their mother let out a laugh. "Oh, boy, have I got stories for her," she said. "Having twins is twice as much everything!"

"What if Steven had a twin brother, too?" Jessica asked. "That would be four times as much everything, wouldn't it?"

Mrs. Wakefield turned around with an astonished expression. "The thought of having two pairs of twins is mind-boggling."

"That's what the reporter thought," Elizabeth mumbled.

Jessica poked Elizabeth with her elbow.

"Well, it will be very nice to be interviewed," Mr. Wakefield said. "I'm just afraid the reporter won't think we're really all that interesting or unusual."

"Oh, yes, she does," Elizabeth mumbled.

Jessica poked Elizabeth again.

"After all, it's really not that uncommon to have twins," Mrs. Wakefield said. "It looked like Casey's was packed with them."

"Unless you have two—" Elizabeth began.

Jessica clamped her hand over Elizabeth's mouth and glared at her. "You promised," she whispered.

"OK, OK," Elizabeth said as they pulled into the driveway.

The moment the car stopped, Steven

42

shoved the door open. "Come on," he said urgently. He beckoned to his sisters.

The twins followed Steven around to the backyard, where they parted some bushes and crawled inside the fort Elizabeth and Jessica had built.

"I know what to do," Steven said as they sat down for a conference.

"What?" Jessica asked.

Steven peeked through the leaves to make sure they were alone. "Here's the plan. When Ms. Loomis is here and asks questions about Bob, we'll change the subject."

"That won't work. We can't change the subject every single time," Elizabeth said.

"Maybe she'll just ask about twins in general," Steven said. "And maybe she won't say anything about two sets of twins."

"But that's why she's coming," Jessica said, sounding doubtful for the first time.

"Well, we'll just have to keep changing the subject," Steven insisted. "Or else let's all talk at once."

Elizabeth frowned. "It just might work," she said slowly. "There's only one problem."

"What?" Steven asked.

"The photographer," Elizabeth said. "Sooner or later we need *two* Stevens."

Jessica bit her lip and Steven frowned. He began stabbing at the dirt with a stick. "We'll think of something before she gets here tomorrow," he said finally.

"Sure," Jessica agreed. "We'll think of something."

"OK," Elizabeth said, feeling deep down that they wouldn't solve the problem. "We'll sleep on it."

"It'll work out," Steven said. "You'll see."

CHAPTER 8

Ms. Loomis Arrives

By the next afternoon Jessica was so nervous she thought she might get sick. They still hadn't solved their biggest problem. They were just going to play it by ear.

"I hope everyone sees our story in the paper," she whispered to Elizabeth as they cleared the lunch dishes from the kitchen table.

"*If* it gets in the paper," Elizabeth whispered back.

"It will, it will," Jessica said.

Steven strolled past them casually.

"Battle stations," he muttered under his breath.

Jessica's eyes widened with alarm. But she was excited, too. She knew it was possible that they might actually pull off part two of their plan without a hitch.

Her heart pounding, Jessica hurried to the living room with Steven. They stood behind the drapes, keeping a lookout for Ms. Loomis. Their parents were in the den, reading the Sunday newspaper and listening to the radio.

Jessica looked over at Steven. He seemed very nervous. He kept jiggling his knee up and down, and looking up and down the street.

"There's a car!" he hissed. "It's slowing down."

"That's her!" Jessica gasped. "Let's go!"

Jessica and Steven raced to the front door, flung it open, and tore outside. They were at the end of the walkway before Ms. Loomis had even stopped at the curb.

"Well, that's a nice welcoming committee!" she called through the open window.

"Hi, Ms. Loomis," Jessica said.

"Now, which ones are you?" the reporter asked with a wide smile.

"Jessica." Jessica gulped. She stared at Steven. "And Bob."

"Everyone else is inside," Steven explained as Ms. Loomis got out of her car. He suddenly snapped his fingers. "I just remembered something. I left my baseball glove in the backyard!"

"Is that important?" Ms. Loomis asked in surprise.

"It's really important!" Steven said seriously. "I'll meet you inside."

Without another word he turned and raced around the side of the house to the backyard. Ms. Loomis took a step up the walkway, but Jessica quickly blocked her.

"It's a nice day, isn't it?" Jessica asked. She had to give Steven time to change from "Bob" to "Steven."

"It's a lovely day," Ms. Loomis replied. She tried to walk around Jessica, but Jessica kept stepping in front of her.

"My parents are really excited to meet you. I like your car," Jessica said, blocking Ms. Loomis.

The reporter gave Jessica a puzzled smile. "Thank you. But aren't we going inside to talk to your parents?"

Jessica gulped. She hoped Steven had had enough time to change his clothes. "Yes. Didn't the photographer come?"

"No, he couldn't," Ms. Loomis said.

Jessica didn't know whether to be relieved or disappointed. "OK, come on," she said, leading the way.

Very slowly, Jessica walked up the path to the front steps. She halted at the bottom of the steps, and Ms. Loomis bumped into her.

"Oh, I'm sorry," Ms. Loomis said, still looking puzzled. "We are going inside, right?"

Jessica took a deep breath. She felt the same way she did whenever she had to jump into a pool at the deep end—a little jittery.

"I just wanted to tie my shoelace," she said, bending over to tie her sneakers.

Ms. Loomis tapped her foot impatiently. At last Jessica stood up. It was now or never.

"Come inside," she said.

At that moment the door opened. Steven came out onto the porch, wearing a different shirt and sneakers instead of flip-flops. His hair was combed differently, too.

"Hi," he said to Ms. Loomis. "I'm Steven."

CHAPTER 9

The Big Interview

Elizabeth stood waiting in the doorway. She doubted Ms. Loomis would actually believe that Steven was two different boys. It might take a few minutes, but wouldn't a reporter be able to detect a trick?

"You must be Elizabeth," Ms. Loomis said.

"Our parents are in the den," Elizabeth told her. She looked down at the ground. "They're expecting you."

The three kids took Ms. Loomis into the den, where they introduced her to their parents.

"We're glad to help you out," Mr. Wakefield said as he shook her hand. "But I'm not so sure you're going to get an interesting story out of us."

"I'm sure you're being modest. Having so many twins must be very interesting," Ms. Loomis said. "It doesn't happen to every family."

Mrs. Wakefield laughed, looking at Elizabeth and Jessica. "They do seem like a lot sometimes, that's true."

Everyone sat down, and Ms. Loomis took out her notebook. She looked around expectantly. "I met Bob outside," she said.

"Bob?" Mrs. Wakefield repeated. "I didn't know he was here."

Elizabeth quickly picked up the dish of mints sitting on the table. "Would you like a candy?" she said to change the subject.

"Oh, thank you," said Ms. Loomis.

"Did you notice that Liz and I are

dressed in matching outfits?" Jessica asked. "We do that a lot. People can't tell us apart then. But my favorite color is pink."

"And mine is green," Elizabeth said quickly.

Ms. Loomis smiled and took some notes. "I noticed you and Bob don't do that," Ms. Loomis said, turning to Steven. "You wear different clothes. Is that because your personalities are very different?"

Steven's eyes widened, and he glanced quickly at their parents before answering. "Umm, no, we don't have much in common, I guess."

"We wouldn't have much trouble telling them apart even if they did," Mr. Wakefield said with a chuckle. "No problem there."

Ms. Loomis looked slightly surprised, but she merely jotted down something on her pad. Elizabeth fidgeted in her seat.

Ms. Loomis still seemed to believe that Steven had a twin brother. So far, so good.

"Tell me about twins," Ms. Loomis said, giving Mrs. Wakefield an encouraging smile. "Does having kids of the same age make being a mother harder or easier?"

"Oh, I'd have to say a little of both," Mrs. Wakefield admitted. "When they were babies, I thought I'd go out of my mind. But then, things like shopping for clothes are simple, because we only have to get one size and the girls can share things around."

"And the boys?" Ms. Loomis asked.

"I've got a really cool science experiment that won a prize at the science fair," Steven broke in hurriedly. "Do you want to see it?"

Ms. Loomis shrugged. "Sure. Did Bob help you with it?"

"Yes, he did," Steven said, which was the truth.

"Bob should have gotten some of the credit for it," Mr. Wakefield said. "He certainly helped Steven a lot. It almost seemed like he lived here for a while."

Ms. Loomis put her pen down and frowned. "Doesn't he?"

"Bob? Of course not," Mr. Wakefield replied.

Ms. Loomis scratched her head. "Where *is* Bob?"

"Is he supposed to be here?" Mrs. Wakefield asked Steven innocently.

Jessica jumped out of her chair and grabbed a pottery vase from a shelf. "I made this at day camp last summer. Do you like it?"

"Very much," Ms. Loomis said.

Elizabeth glanced nervously at her brother. She could tell that the reporter was getting more and more suspicious with every minute.

"I guess you must attract a certain

56

amount of attention when you have twins, is that right?" Ms. Loomis went on. There was a frown on her forehead, as though she was trying very hard to figure something out.

"They don't get so much attention around town here," Mrs. Wakefield explained. "So many people in Sweet Valley know our family. But when we go on vacations, they do turn heads."

"With four, I should say so," Ms. Loomis said.

"Four?" Mr. Wakefield repeated.

"Four kids," Ms. Loomis said, her frown deepening.

"No, just three," Mrs. Wakefield said. She was beginning to look puzzled, too. "The girls and Steven."

Ms. Loomis opened her eyes very wide. "Doesn't Bob go with you on family trips?"

"Oh, no," Mr. Wakefield said. "We think

he's a nice boy, and sometimes we invite him along to keep Steven company, but we don't include him in all of our family activities."

"You don't?" Ms. Loomis asked in a shocked voice.

"No, of course not," Mrs. Wakefield said.

Ms. Loomis nodded as she wrote. "But doesn't he feel left out?"

Mrs. Wakefield looked at Mr. Wakefield, then back at Ms. Loomis. "Well, I certainly don't mean for him to."

Elizabeth felt her face grow red. The reporter must believe the Wakefields were either crazy or cruel. Whatever the article said, it wouldn't make her family sound very nice.

She scooted over to Jessica. "We have to tell the truth," she whispered into Jessica's ear.

"No," Jessica whispered. "It's working fine. She believes it."

That was what Elizabeth was afraid of. She watched Ms. Loomis writing in the notebook. Steven stood up and dug his hands into his pockets.

"Well, I can't stay," he said. "Bob and I have a baseball game over at the park."

"I didn't get much of a chance to talk to Bob at all," Ms. Loomis complained. "He went to get his baseball glove, and that's the last I saw of him."

"It's not that important for your article, though," Mr. Wakefield pointed out.

"If you say so," Ms. Loomis said in a doubtful voice. She looked at Steven and reached into her shoulder bag. "But before you two leave, can I at least get a photograph?"

The reporter pulled out a camera, and Elizabeth felt her heart sink into her sneakers.

CHAPTER 10

Picture Time

"Great idea," Mrs. Wakefield said. "A family portrait."

"Oh, we don't really have to get our picture taken, do we?" Elizabeth asked in a worried voice.

Jessica felt trapped. She wanted her picture in the paper. But if Ms. Loomis wanted Bob in the picture, then the truth was sure to come out.

And then she definitely wouldn't get her picture in the paper.

"Where would you like us to sit or stand?" Mr. Wakefield asked.

"Maybe on the front steps of the house," Ms. Loomis suggested. "It's nice and bright outside."

"Come on, kids," Mrs. Wakefield said, standing up and shooing the twins and Steven ahead of her.

"What are we going to do?" Jessica whispered to Elizabeth as they hurried to the door.

"I don't know," Elizabeth said. "I told you something stupid would happen. I told you!"

Mr. and Mrs. Wakefield led the way outside and stood in front of the door. Ms. Loomis walked down the steps and then turned to focus her camera.

Jessica held her breath. She prayed that Ms. Loomis would just forgot about Bob. Then everything would work out fine.

"We're ready when you are," Mrs. Wakefield said with a wide smile.

Ms. Loomis lowered the camera. "Jessica, could you go find your other brother?"

Jessica froze. Steven froze. Elizabeth slowly shook her head.

"Other brother?" Mrs. Wakefield asked. She frowned at the kids. "*Other* brother?"

"Umm . . . ," Jessica stammered.

Steven gulped. "Umm . . ."

"Well, you see—" Elizabeth began.

"It was all—" Jessica said at the same time.

"We were just trying—" Steven blurted out with them.

"Hang on!" Ms. Loomis crossed her arms across her chest. "What kind of joke is this?"

At that moment they all heard the whirring of bicycle wheels. A skinny, red-haired, freckled boy with bright-blue eyes rode up the driveway and jumped off his bike. "Hi, everyone!" he called.

"Oh, no!" Jessica said, letting out a

huge sigh. "What rotten timing."

"Hi, Bob," Mr. Wakefield said.

"Bob?" Ms. Loomis repeated. "You're not Bob."

Steven sat down on the step and put his head in his hands. "Yes, he is," he muttered.

Everyone was silent. Bob, Ms. Loomis, and Mr. and Mrs. Wakefield all looked very confused. After a long, puzzled pause Elizabeth broke the silence by bursting into laughter.

Then Jessica began to giggle, too, and Steven laughed so hard he almost fell off the step.

"We—we—" Steven tried to say.

"You're not identical twins, are you?" Ms. Loomis accused Bob.

Bob shrugged. "What are you talking about?"

Jessica laughed even harder at that. "He's not even our brother!"

"Will someone please explain what is going on here?" Mr. Wakefield demanded.

Instantly Jessica, Elizabeth, and Steven stopped laughing. Jessica wasn't sure if she had laughed because their joke was so funny, or because she was so nervous. For the moment she took a step closer to Elizabeth.

"Well, it all started yesterday," Steven explained, his face turning pink. "I wanted to see if I could get a Twin Delight, so I pretended I was a twin."

"But Bob doesn't look anything like you," Mrs. Wakefield exclaimed.

Jessica nodded. "He wasn't there. Steven pretended to be two people. He said he had a twin brother named Bob."

"And then Ms. Loomis wanted to interview us because she thought we had two sets of twins in the same family," Elizabeth added.

66

Ms. Loomis had stared in disbelief as the kids explained the mystery. At last, she let out a good-natured laugh.

"Well, no wonder!" she said. "I thought you were the most heartless family!"

Mrs. Wakefield looked very embarrassed. "Oh, dear! All those questions. You thought we had a son named Bob whom we didn't care about. This is so embarrassing." She turned and glared at Steven and the twins, but then she spoiled it by laughing.

"I still don't get it," Bob said in a puzzled voice.

At that everyone began to laugh all over again. Jessica felt a wave of relief wash over her. It didn't look as if they would get into trouble, after all.

"I guess you don't have a story for the newspaper, Ms. Loomis," Mrs. Wakefield said.

The reporter shook her head. "No, but I

have a great story to tell my friends."

"And I think you have a story to tell the manager of the ice-cream shop," Mr. Wakefield told Steven.

Steven looked sheepish. "I know. I was going to pay for the sundaes anyway."

"He just wanted a Twin Delight—badly," Jessica explained.

"Twin Delight—that's what I've got," Mrs. Wakefield said with a laugh. "But one pair of twins is all the delight I need."

Jessica and Elizabeth were playing in the park with Ellen Riteman and Eva Simpson later that afternoon. They had told their friends what had happened at Casey's yesterday and with Ms. Loomis earlier.

"I can't believe your parents didn't ground you and Steven forever," Ellen said. She was a good friend of Jessica's and had been the first one to tell the twins about Casey's Twin Sundae Delight.

"Yeah, but I bet it was a funny joke," Eva said in her pretty singsongy voice. She had moved to Sweet Valley from Jamaica, an island in the Caribbean, many months ago. Everyone liked her a lot.

"Mom and Dad were mad, but they laughed too," Jessica said. "Besides, Steven paid Mr. Bixby for the two free sundaes he got."

"So everything's back to normal," Elizabeth said. "We don't have to be scared of going back to Casey's."

"Good, because when we go together, I'm going to order a triple scoop of pistachio on a cone," Eva said. She licked her lips just thinking about it.

"And I'm going to . . . uh-oh, here comes Lois," Ellen said. She pointed at

Lois Waller, who was pedaling her bicycle toward them. "Lois sure doesn't need to eat any more ice cream."

Lois was in the girls' second-grade class. She was chubby, and a lot of kids made fun of her. It didn't help that Lois was shy. Still, Jessica, Elizabeth, Ellen, and Eva always tried to be nice to her.

"Hi, Lois," Elizabeth said when Lois stopped in front of them. "We're going to play tag in a little bit. Jessica's going to be it. Do you want to play?"

"I'd like to, but it's already five," Lois said, looking at the tall clock in the middle of the park. "My mom told me to be home by now. I'm late. I just wanted to say hi."

Jessica shook her head. "Your mom always makes you come home early," she said.

"I . . . I know," Lois said, looking down

at the ground. "But I've got to go." She quickly pedaled off.

"Poor Lois," Elizabeth said. "She misses out on a lot of fun."

Will Lois ever be part of the fun? Find out in Sweet Valley Kids #51, LOIS AND THE SLEEPOVER.

SIGN UP FOR THE SWEET VALLEY HIGH® FAN CLUB!

Hey, girls! Get all the gossip on Sweet Valley High's® most popular teenagers when you join our fantastic Fan Club! As a member, you'll get all of this really cool stuff:

- Membership Card with your own personal Fan Club ID number
- A Sweet Valley High® Secret Treasure Box
- Sweet Valley High® Stationery
- Official Fan Club Pencil (for secret note writing!)
- Three Bookmarks
- A "Members Only" Door Hanger
- Two Skeins of J. & P. Coats® Embroidery Floss with flower barrette instruction leaflet
- Two editions of *The Oracle* newsletter
- Plus exclusive Sweet Valley High® product offers, special savings, contests, and much more!

Be the first to find out what Jessica & Elizabeth Wakefield are up to by joining the Sweet Valley High® Fan Club for the one-year membership fee of only $6.25 each for U.S. residents, $8.25 for Canadian residents (U.S. currency). Includes shipping & handling.

Send a check or money order (do not send cash) made payable to "Sweet Valley High® Fan Club" along with this form to:

SWEET VALLEY HIGH® FAN CLUB, BOX 3919-B, SCHAUMBURG, IL 60168-3919

NAME_____
(Please print clearly)

ADDRESS_____

CITY_____ STATE_____ ZIP_____
(Required)

AGE_____ BIRTHDAY_____ /_____ /_____

SWEET VALLEY KIDS

Jessica and Elizabeth have had lots of adventures in *Sweet Valley High* and *Sweet Valley Twins*...now read about the twins at age seven! You'll love all the fun that comes with being seven—birthday parties, playing dress-up, class projects, putting on puppet shows and plays, losing a tooth, setting up lemonade stands, caring for animals and much more! It's all part of SWEET VALLEY KIDS. Read them all!